D0467102

'18

Dear Parents and Educators,

Welcome to Penguin Young Readers! As parents and educators, you know that each child develops at his or her own pace—in terms of speech, critical thinking, and, of course, reading. Penguin Young Readers recognizes this fact. As a result, each Penguin Young Readers book is assigned a traditional easy-to-read level (1–4) as well as a Guided Reading Level (A–P). Both of these systems will help you choose the right book for your child. Please refer to the back of each book for specific leveling information. Penguin Young Readers features esteemed authors and illustrators, stories about favorite characters, fascinating nonfiction, and more!

Mo Jackson: Kick It, Mo!

LEVEL **2**

GUIDED
READING
LEVEL **I**

This book is perfect for a **Progressing Reader** who:
• can figure out unknown words by using picture and context clues;
• can recognize beginning, middle, and ending sounds;
• can make and confirm predictions about what will happen in the text; and
• can distinguish between fiction and nonfiction.

Here are some **activities** you can do during and after reading this book:
• Word Repetition: Reread the story and count how many times you read the following words: kick, ball, ground, and goal. Then, on a separate sheet of paper, work with the child to write a new sentence for each word.
• Summarize: Work with the child to write a short summary about what happened in the story. What happened in the beginning? What happened in the middle? What happened at the end?

Remember, sharing the love of reading with a child is the best gift you can give!

—Sarah Fabiny, Editorial Director
  Penguin Young Readers program

*Penguin Young Readers are leveled by independent reviewers applying the standards developed by Irene Fountas and Gay Su Pinnell in *Matching Books to Readers: Using Leveled Books in Guided Reading*, Heinemann, 1999.

For my ever-lovely wife Renée —D.A.A.

For Marston —S.R.

Penguin Young Readers
An imprint of Penguin Random House LLC
375 Hudson Street
New York, New York 10014

First published in the United States of America by Penguin Young Readers,
an imprint of Penguin Random House LLC, 2018

Text copyright © 2018 by David Adler
Illustrations copyright © 2018 by Sam Ricks

LIBRARY OF CONGRESS CATALOGING-IN-PUBLICATION DATA IS AVAILABLE
ISBN: 9780425289815

Printed in China

1 3 5 7 9 10 8 6 4 2

KICK IT, MO!

by David A. Adler
illustrated by Sam Ricks

Penguin Young Readers
An Imprint of Penguin Random House LLC

"Kick it! Kick the ball!"

Mo Jackson calls out.

Mo kicks his desk.

"Kick it! Kick the ball!"

Mo kicks his bed.

"Kick it! Kick the ball!"

Mo kicks his pillow.

The pillow flies

into the hall.

Crash!

"Hey! You knocked over some books," his mother tells him.

"I'm sorry," Mo says.

"But I need to practice. I have a soccer game today. I need to kick, kick, kick."

Mo and his mother and father
pick up the books.
They all go outside.
Mo's mother rolls a soccer ball
and Mo kicks it.

But he kicks it

high into the air.

"Kick it low,"

his father tells him.

"Kick it on the ground."

Mo kicks the ball again.

It flies behind him.

Mo's mom and dad roll the

ball again and again.

Mo kicks it again and again.

But mostly he does not kick it

on the ground.

They all go to the soccer field.

Mo's team is the Billy Goats.

They are playing the Pups.

Mo is smaller and younger

than all the other players.

Coach Judy tells Mo's team,

"Keep the ball low.

Kick it on the ground.

Kick it toward the goal."

Tweet! Tweet!

The game starts.

The other team, the Pups,

has the ball.

A big Pups player

kicks it hard.

The ball speeds past Mo.

Mo chases after it.

A big Billy Goats player

kicks it the other way.

Mo stops.

He turns.

He runs the

other way.

The ball goes one way.

It goes the other way.

Mo runs after the ball.

He runs back and forth.

At last Mo stops.

He is tired.

The game is almost over.

The score is tied

zero to zero.

Mo is very close to the Pups' goal.

The ball stops by Mo.

"Kick the ball!

Kick the ball!"

Coach Judy shouts.

Mo pulls his foot back.

He is about to kick the ball.

A big Pups player

gets in front of Mo and kicks it.

Mo watches the ball

speed down the field toward

the Billy Goats' goal.

Mo is too tired

to chase it.

A Pups player kicks the ball

right at the goal.

The Billy Goats goalie catches it.

She throws it back onto the field.

No score!

A Billy Goats player

kicks the ball hard.

It rolls toward the goal.

"Yes!" Mo shouts.

He thinks his team will score.

But the Pups goalie stops it.

He throws it hard.

He throws it right at Mo.

Mo pulls his foot way back.

It's a mighty kick.

The Pups goalie jumps.

But Mo's mighty kick

mostly misses the ball.

The ball rolls slowly into the goal.

"Yes!" Coach Judy shouts.

"Goal!" Billy Goats players shout.

Tweet! Tweet!

The game is over.

The Billy Goats win one to zero.

"Mo! Mo! Mo!"

the Billy Goats shout.

Mo tells Coach Judy,

"But I missed my kick."

Coach Judy says,

"You fooled the goalie.

He jumped for a hard, high kick,

but you kept the ball on the

ground."